Emmy
and the
Plastic Pond

Nick Garlick

DEDICATION

For

Matt & Houriya
Zachary & Sophia

Faraway friends

Contents

1   A New Friend

Emmy was new at school and nobody liked her.

They didn't like her because she smelled bad.

The reason she smelled bad was the Blascoe
Brothers. The three of them stopped her on the steps
on her very first day and blocked the door so she
couldn't get in. They were standing on the top step, so
she had to crane her neck all the way back to look up at
them. It made her feel very small and nervous.

Even so, she did her best to be polite. Emmy
was always polite.

'Hello,' she said. 'I'm Emmy. Who are you?'

'Bash Blascoe,' the boy in the middle
announced. He pointed to the other two. 'That's Brick
and he's Bang. We're brothers. We made our own
names up. And we've got a present for you.'

He lobbed a paper bag at her. Emmy caught it with both hands. The paper was wet and soggy and it broke the moment she touched it. As the contents splashed down her front from her chin to her knees, Bash, Brick and Bang ran off laughing.

Emmy tried furiously to scrape the ghastly, foul mess off her clothes. It smelt of vinegar and rotten eggs and the mud you find in the bottom of a bucket that hasn't been emptied in years.

It was *awful*.

Everybody in her new class agreed. They all held their noses and made a big show of not going *anywhere* near her. And since no amount of soap and water could get rid of the smell, in the end her teachers told her she could go home and change her clothes and come back the next day.

She did, only to discover that things were just as

bad. When she arrived at school, the Blascoe Brothers were waiting to greet her. They held their noses and called out 'Eeeeeuuuugghhh! What a stink! Keep away from Smelly Emmy!'

That was all it took. Wherever she went that day, everybody she saw made a big show of holding their noses and calling out Smelly Emmy.

All except Samira. She sat next to Emmy in class and the Blascoe Brothers teased her too. They called her Soppy Sammy. They liked to tease her after class by snatching something from her and tossing it back and forth over her head. She was never quick enough to grab it.

But Emmy was. On her third day at school, she crept up quietly, unseen and unnoticed, and when Bash tossed the object to Bang, she plucked it from the air and ran. The brothers were shocked. They didn't know whether to chase Emmy or tease Samira. By the time they'd decided, both girls were gone.

Emmy handed over the object she'd rescued. It was a nasal spray.

'Thank you,' Samira said, taking two deep sniffs from the little plastic bottle. 'I have hay fever. This helps keep my nose clear. But because of all the sniffs, the Blascoe Brothers call me *Soppy Sammy*.'

'They're terrible bullies,' Emmy said.

Samira agreed. 'They didn't used to be. They were nice once. But not anymore. Now they just love being mean. And that's why everyone else is making fun of you. Because if they make fun of you, the brothers won't bully *them*.'

The two girls, now firm friends, walked on until they reached the bottom of the road where they both lived.

Where they stopped and stared at the saddest

sight either of them had ever seen.

2   A Sad Sight

They were standing at the entrance to a small park. It lay at the end of the street where they both lived and it had been terribly neglected. The paint on the gates was flaking. The grass was patchy and ragged. But the saddest part was the pond.

It was shaped like an egg, with a small island in the middle. A solitary tree grew on the island. Its drooping branches were thick with scraps of old plastic shopping bags. They fluttered listlessly in the breeze.

The pond was even worse. Its entire surface was covered in a thick green blanket of duckweed. Sticking up out of this blanket were four rusty shopping trolleys, several battered plastic crates and dozens of empty drink cans. Stuck in the mud at the edges were more plastic bags than either girl could count.

'This is *awful*,' Emmy said.

Samira nodded. 'It's been like this for ages.'

'Why doesn't somebody clean it up?'

Before Samira could answer, her mum appeared and called her inside. So Emmy went home and asked her Uncle Glum.

That wasn't his real name, of course. His real name was Alexander Appleby. He lived all on his own in an old lighthouse at the top of a cliff, overlooking the small seaside town he'd made his home. He never smiled. He rarely spoke. He shuffled around in his dressing gown and slippers and spent all day watching the telly.

He hadn't always been like this. He'd been married once, to Emmy's Aunt Evie, a woman who loved to laugh and go sailing. But one day, a year before, she'd taken her boat out by herself and been swept away forever by a terrible storm. Uncle Alex had never recovered.

Emmy was living with him temporarily, while her mum and dad were far away at work, helping to protect a family of gorillas in a tropical rain forest. They'd thought looking after Emmy might cheer him up a little.

And Emmy did her best. She was quiet and tidy. She helped with the shopping and watered the plants in his garden. She even learned to make his favourite food: toasted cheese sandwiches.

But it didn't help.

Uncle Alex remained Uncle Glum.

Even so, he wasn't unkind. The house was warm, there was always plenty of food in the cupboards, and he'd given her the best room of all, right at the top with a terrific view of the sea. Once it had been his bedroom, but he didn't like to look at the sea any more. It reminded him of what had happened to Aunt Evie and made him sad. He slept downstairs at the back of the house, in a room where the curtains were always drawn.

He was sitting in there when she got home. She told him what she'd seen in the park.

'I know,' he sighed when she finished. 'Somebody ought to do something, I suppose...'

His voice faded away and he went back to watching TV. He didn't say another word for the rest of the day, except to murmur 'Good night,' when Emmy went to bed.

As she put on her pyjamas, she saw storm clouds gathering out at sea. When she climbed under the covers, the first drops of rain began to spatter against the glass. She snuggled down and drifted off to sleep, only to wake up in the middle of the night when

she heard tapping on the glass.

What she saw when she did made her scream.

3   Into the Storm

Peering in through the glass was a little girl. She was no bigger than Emmy. Her face was pale. Her eyes were wide and round. Long red hair flowed to her waist and around a thin blue dress.

Emmy shook her head. It was impossible for the girl to be where she was, because the only thing outside the window was a raging sea crashing against the cliffs below the house. There was nothing for her to be standing on.

She opened her mouth to scream again but the little girl stopped her.

'Oh, don't do that,' she said. 'It's not nice.'

'It's not nice seeing a ghost,' Emmy said.

'Who says I'm a ghost?' the little girl demanded.

'You're standing on thin air outside my window

above a stormy sea,' Emmy said. 'What else could you be *except* a ghost?'

'Oh, don't be so silly,' said the girl, looking exasperated at such foolishness. 'I'm a water sprite. You can call me Ariel. It's one of my favourite names.'

The wind howled. The rain hammered down. Far below Emmy's window, giant waves thundered against the rocks with such force the whole house trembled.

None of this made Ariel so much as blink. She didn't even look wet.

'What are you *doing* out there?' Emmy asked. She wasn't scared any more. But she *was* really puzzled.

'Looking for you,' Ariel said.

'Me?' Emmy said. 'Why?'

'Because I've come to show you.'

'Show me what?'

Ariel pointed at the sea.

'I've already seen it,' Emmy said. 'I see it every day.'

'I know *that*,' Ariel said, grabbing her wrist and pulling her right through the glass as though it didn't exist. 'But you haven't seen it from where *I'm* taking you.'

The next thing she knew, Emmy and Ariel were flying downwards, straight into the teeth of the raging waves.

4   Bullies

The wind howled. The rain lashed down. Emmy heard voices. It was the waves, talking.

'You're going to get it now,' one growled.

'We're going to bash you to bits,' roared a second.

'Crunching up water sprites and their friends is *so* much fun,' thundered a third.

'Not a chance!' Ariel yelled back as she plunged into the water.

And she was right. The two girls slipped away from the waves as easily as tiny birds flitting through the branches of a forest. Within seconds the turbulent surface had faded from view. The water grew still. Down and down they glided, into the dark silent depths of the ocean.

'How did you *do* that?' Emmy asked.

'Oh, storm waves are terrible bullies,' Ariel said. 'They're always shouting and roaring and making tons of noise. I just ignore them. Then they don't know what to do. They get terribly confused.'

'I know bullies at school,' Emmy said. 'They scare me.'

'Do you ignore them?'

'No.'

'You should. Works wonders. Now don't dawdle. We've got to hurry. There's tons to see.'

Emmy was getting more confused by the second. 'Tons to see of *what*?' she asked.

'My world,' said Ariel. 'And all my friends.'

On they flew.

5   Terrified!

They swooped through massive canyons. They flew over sprawling plains dotted with rocks and the rusting hulks of sunken ships. Shoals of fish darted. Coral reefs glittered with a thousand colours.

The colour of the sea changed constantly. One moment it was a deep, deep blue that was almost black. A moment later it was a bright glistening turquoise, shimmering over blinding white sands. Dolphins curled around them, cackling happily as they kept the travellers company. Finally it turned blue, a cold hard blue dotted with drifting chunks of white as big as a building.

'Icebergs,' Ariel called out. 'Mind you don't bump your head.'

Seals whooshed by looking for supper. Penguins

darted past as fast as bullets.

Ariel stopped. The two of them settled on the tip of an undersea mountain.

'What are we doing?' Emmy asked.

'Waiting,' the sprite said.

'For what?'

Ariel put her finger to her lips. Emmy was startled, because it wasn't a finger any more. It was a long thing strip of plastic. Like all her other fingers. All of them were made of plastic.

'What's happened to you?' she asked.

Ariel didn't answer. Instead she pointed.

A long, silver blue fish emerged from the gloom. Emmy recognized it immediately. It was a shark. Her whole body went rigid with fear and, once again, she was sure she was about to be eaten. Yet all the shark did was glide around them in slow lazy circles before slipping back into the darkness.

Ariel smiled. 'Did you recognize it?' she asked.

Emmy didn't answer. She was too terrified to
talk.

'It was a Greenland shark,' Ariel said. 'Or to give
it it's Greenlandic name, *Eqalussuaq*. They're very rare,
you know. They only swim in these waters. They like the
cold and the deep.'

Finally, Emmy found her voice. 'Why weren't
you *scared*?'

'Why should I be scared?'

'It was a *shark*! Didn't you see its teeth? It
looked awful!'

'Rubbish,' said Ariel. 'He's a friend of mine. And
besides, you probably look awful to him. You can't tell
just by looking at someone. Now,' she continued, 'if I
was going to be scared of anything, I suppose I might be

scared of what's on its way.'

While they'd been talking, the sea around them had filled with thousands, possibly even millions of tiny silver, shrimp-like creatures flecked with red. Emmy could see nothing else. But they only tickled when they touched her. They certainly didn't scare her and she said so.

'Oh,' said Ariel, 'I didn't mean *them*. I meant *that*.'

From out of the depths loomed a blue-grey shadow. A mouth so wide it could have swallowed a train swung open. Emmy saw row upon row of needle-like teeth.

'I just *love* this bit,' Ariel said with a giggle.

Emmy didn't. She clawed desperately at the water, trying to get away. But the current was too strong. She couldn't escape its grip. Head over heels, she tumbled into the gaping mouth. Ariel went with her, both of them surrounded by a cloud of the tiny red and silver creatures. The mouth swung shut and darkness descended.

Then she was flying backwards, back the way she'd come, bouncing and banging her way between the rows of teeth and out into the ocean. Head spinning, she whirled over and over as the blue-grey shadow glided past her for what seemed like hours until, with one flick of its mighty tail fin, it vanished into the depths.

Ariel floated up beside her, grinning from ear to ear.

'Wasn't that *fun*!' she beamed.

Emmy was dizzy. She was seeing two of everything. 'What was that?' she gasped.

'We got swallowed by a whale,' Ariel said. 'A

blue whale. The largest animal on the planet.'

'I thought it was going to eat us! With those horrible teeth!'

Ariel shook her head. 'They weren't teeth. They were baleen plates. The whale takes in a ginormous mouthful of water, which is packed with krill. That's those little fish that were swimming all around us. Then, when it absolutely can't swallow any more, it pushes all that water back out through the plates.'

'What happens to the krill?'

'They can't get past the plates. They stay inside. They're what the whale feeds on. Gajillions of them.'

Emmy was more confused than ever. 'Then why didn't it eat *us*? We're even bigger than the krill. If *they* couldn't get through the plates, why did we?'

Ariel shook her head. 'Haven't you worked it out yet?'

'Worked out what?'

'The plates stop the krill, but water passes through them. Just like *we* passed through them.'

'So?'

Ariel floated before her. With a shake of her long flowing hair, she broke apart into thousands of minute drops that swirled back and forth like a cloud. As Emmy watched, open-mouthed, they drew together again, into Ariel.

'You're – Emmy began.

'Water!' Ariel said. 'Every single minute drop of me. One hundred percent water. So top marks to you. Straight to the head of the class. An *excellent* end-of-term report. But no time for talking. Still tons to see.'

She grabbed Emmy's hand and stepped into a passing deep-sea current.

Away they went again.

6   Names

They zoomed past a forest of giant white tubes, waving and swirling. Rocks glowed red as lava pulsed from deep in the core of the Earth. A current of hot air grabbed them and sent them spinning head over heels up through the darkness towards the light.

'That's another good bit,' Ariel called out over her shoulder. She giggled. 'The heat makes my toes go all tingly.'

A school of strange spiky creatures flashed by, eyes bulging and fins glittering.

'Pacific!' they called out. 'Nice to see you.'

'Nice to see you too,' Ariel replied.

Emmy was puzzled. 'I thought you said your name was Ariel.'

'It is.'

'But they called you Pacific.'

'Oh, I've got *lots* of names,' Ariel said. 'Ariel's just my favourite.'

'What are the others?'

'Ocean,' Ariel said. 'Reservoir. Lake, loch, pond. Stream, rivulet, creek. Lagoon and puddle. That's ten. And just in English. There's *lac* in French, *meer* in Dutch, *göl* in Turkish and 温德米尔湖 in Chinese. Actually, that last one's cheating. It's *Lake Windermere* in Mandarin. Have you ever been there? It's lovely. The tourists trail their fingers over the side of the boat and tickle me all along my back. Did you know –'

Emmy interrupted. She pointed at Ariel's feet. The right one had turned into a plastic bottle. The left one was now an old crumpled coffee cup..

'What's *happening* to you?' she said

Ariel shrugged. 'Occupational hazard,' she said.

'It's not easy being water, you know. Not these days.'

'But –'

Ariel cut her off. 'No time to talk. Still a lot to see. Otherwise you won't know what to do.'

'Do?' asked Emmy. 'What have I got to do?'

Ariel didn't answer. She was breaking apart again.

They *both* were.

7   Transformation

Just like Ariel, Emmy's body was dissolving into thousands of tiny droplets as fine as mist. Ariel let out a whoop of delight and pointed upwards.

'Here we go!' she cried.

The two of them broke loose from the surface of the sea and floated into the air. Above them, thick white clouds beckoned. Soon they were enveloped in white. It caressed and cocooned them.

Ariel pointed downwards. 'Great view,' she said.

Emmy gazed at the ocean far, far below. As she watched it became land, then mountains. Around them the clouds began to churn and grow darker. The two girls were buffeted from side to side.

'Just getting ready to fall,' Ariel said. 'Nothing to worry about.'

Despite all that had happened on this strange wild journey, Emmy's heart leapt into her throat at this latest information. '*Fall*?' she croaked.

'Part of the process,' Ariel smiled and took Emmy's hand with her plastic fingers.

Then they fell, into darkness and gusts of wind that blew them in all directions. Lightning cracked. Thunder rumbled. They tumbled past the jagged peaks of mighty mountains, past forests of green and brown and landed with a splash in a shallow pool between two rocks.

From the pool they drifted into a stream. The stream flowed into a river. The river became a raging torrent, bashing and breaking against rocks as it raced on its way to the sea. The two of them were swept over the lip of a mighty waterfall and landed in the churning waters at the base. Tender fingers swept them up and eased them into calmer waters.

'Nice to see you, Ariel,' said a voice. 'You have a *wonderful* day now!'

'That was Niagara,' Ariel said. 'Such a friendly waterfall. I've got a sister who prefers Iguaçu though, all the way down in Brazil. You get a free massage there.'

Emmy wasn't really listening. She was too busy staring at what Ariel had become.

The water sprite was back in one piece again, but she didn't look anything like the figure who'd appeared at Emmy's bedroom window. Now it wasn't just her fingers and her feet that were made of plastic. Her long, flowing, beautiful hair been replaced by a tangle of bent and battered drinking straws.

'What's *happened* to you?' Emmy said.

'I told you,' Ariel said with a little shrug. 'Occupational hazard.'

'But why?' Emmy cried. '*How*?'

'People drop rubbish,' Ariel said. 'They just throw it away, wherever they are. They don't clean up after themselves. But we're used to it.'

'Who's *we*?' Emmy asked.

'My family,' said Ariel. 'All of us. Ponds and reservoirs. Lakes and lochs. Rivers and waterfalls and rapids and oceans and clouds and rain. We're all related, you know. We come in countless forms, but we all belong to one big, huge, vast family.'

'Water, 'said Emmy.

'That's right,' said Ariel. 'Water. Straight to the top of the class again.' But there was no joy now in her words or her voice. 'And here we are.'

'Where?' asked Emmy.

Ariel spread her plastic fingers wide. 'Back where we started,' she said. 'Or almost.'

Emmy looked.

And her heart sank even further.

8   A Plea

They were in the pond in the park at the bottom of the street where Emmy and Samira lived. The two of them were drifting sluggishly back and forth amongst the empty cans, the rusting shopping trolleys and the plastic crates. Beside her, Ariel was now completely transformed.

Her eyes were bottle tops. Her nose was a toothpaste cap. Her legs and arms were ragged shopping bags and her torso was a knot of greasy fast-food boxes.

'You have to help me, Emmy,' she said, through lips made of plastic wrapping. 'Help my family.'

'Help? Emmy said. 'How?'

'Make me clean. Make us all clean.'

'But I'm too little! There's only me. I can't clean

39

all the water!'

'Then do what you can,' Ariel whispered. 'Do what you can.'

They were the last words she spoke. As soon as they were out of her mouth, she began to break apart. Emmy struggled to her side, to enfold her in her arms and comfort her.

She was too late.

By the time she reached her, there was nothing to see but a puddle of bags and straws and bottle tops, spread out across the surface of the pond like a stain.

And now Emmy herself was sinking.

Filthy water crept up her body. It slopped over her shoulders and trickled into her mouth. She flailed her arms wildly, searching for something solid to hold onto, but all she found was rubbish.

She was sinking, and there was nothing she

could do about it.

The last thing she heard, as she slipped beneath

the surface with a plastic bag wrapped around her

head, was Ariel's voice, fainter than ever.

'Help me, Emmy. Help us all!'

9   Just a Dream

Emmy opened her eyes, only to find she couldn't see a thing. Just as she began to panic, gentle hands reached out to calm her. Then bright morning sunlight spilled into her eyes and she saw her uncle sitting beside her.

'It's all right,' he said. 'You were just having a nightmare. You had your head *inside* the pillowcase and your legs all tangled in the duvet. You sounded very scared.'

'I was,' Emmy said. She could still recall every single second of the ghastly way the dream had ended. It made her shiver.

'What was it about?' he asked.

'I had a friend,' Emmy said. 'And she vanished. I couldn't save her.'

As soon as the words were out of her mouth, Emmy wished she'd kept quiet. Uncle Glum's sad eyes turned even sadder than usual, and she knew he was thinking about Aunt Evie, and how he hadn't been able to save *her*.

Then he smiled. It was a sad smile, to be sure, and over almost before it began, but it was still a smile. He brushed the hair from her eyes.

'Well,' he said, 'you're all safe now. 'And it's time for breakfast. *And* it's Saturday today, so there's no school. You can do what you want.'

'I'd like to go to the park,' Emmy said. She couldn't forget her dream, and even though it *was* just a dream, she felt compelled to go and see if Ariel was there. 'Would you like to come too?'

Uncle Glum gave her a sad smile and shook his head. 'No,' he said. 'I think I'll stay inside today. But you can go. As long as you're careful.'

'I promise,' Emmy said

'And come right home if there's any trouble.'

'I promise that too,' she said.

She got dressed, ate her breakfast, grabbed her boots and set off at a run.

To the pond.

10 Earl

It looked the same as it always did.

The water was choked with duckweed and littered with shopping trolleys and crates and cans. After the storm in the night, the tree on the little island in the middle had acquired even more ragged plastic bags to adorn its branches.

But there was no sign of Ariel. Not that she'd *really* expected to find her. After all, it had been a dream, hadn't it?

She saw a man from the council by the gates. He was emptying a rubbish bin. She went over to talk to him.

'Hello,' she said. 'May I ask you a question?'

He stopped what he was doing and turned towards her. 'Of course you may.'

'Why doesn't anybody do anything to clean the pond?'

The man frowned. He looked as sad as Emmy felt. 'No money,' he said. 'The council can't afford to clean it up.'

'But you're emptying the bins,' Emmy said. 'Isn't somebody paying *you*?'

'They *are*,' he said with a wry smile, 'but only to empty the bins. And even then I have to work on my day off just to keep up, because there's only me. I haven't got the time to keep the *park* clean, let alone the pond.'

He took out a handkerchief and wiped his forehead. It was a hot morning and he was already sweating. He was obviously working very hard.

That's when Emmy had an idea.

'Could *I* tidy it up?'

'You?' said the man from the council.

'A little bit, at least. Even if I only pick up some of the rubbish, just the bits stuck in the mud at the edge, it would make a difference, wouldn't it? It would be better than nothing. And I wouldn't get wet.' She pointed at her feet. 'I've already got my wellington boots on.'

The man from the council thought it over.

'Well,' he said, 'if you promise to be careful and not to fall in, then *I'll* help *you*. A little bit.' He walked over to his van and returned with some rubbish bags. He handed them to Emmy. 'If you fill those up and tie them neatly and put them there by the gates, *I'll* come back when I've finished my work and collect them. How does that sound?'

'It sounds great,' Emmy said, taking the bags.

'And,' he continued, going back to rummage

around inside his van, 'you'd better have these.' He handed her an old pair of gardening gloves. 'They'll help keep your hands clean. It's a very *dirty* pond.'

Emmy took them and pulled them on. They were a bit big, but not too much. She could still pick things up with them.

'Thank you,' she said. 'My name's Emmy, by the way.'

The man from the council took off his glove and held out his hand. 'It's very nice to meet you, Emmy. My name's Earl.'

They shook hands. Then Earl climbed back into his van and Emmy watched him drive away.

Snapping open a bag, she turned to face the pond.

11   The Clean-up Begins

It was much harder work than she'd expected. Before she was even halfway round the pond, the bag was so full she had to drag it along the ground behind her.

And it was dirty.

Really dirty.

Into the bag went fast food containers, drink cans, plastic bottles, shopping bags and old soggy newspapers. She was glad Earl had lent her the gloves, because some of the rubbish she picked up was so old and filthy she wouldn't have dared touch it with her bare hands.

When the first bag was full, she propped it against a bench, snapped open the second and started to fill that. When that was full, she opened a third bag and kept going. When they were *all* full, she dragged them up to the gates and tried to tie them shut.

That was when she encountered a new problem.

Before she could tie a knot in the ends of the bag, she had to push the rubbish down inside it so there was enough plastic at the top to *make* a knot. That part was easy. She just knelt on it. But the moment she stood up to tie the knot, and took her weight off the rubbish, it all swelled up to the top again.

Nothing she tried worked.

She was stumped.

Yet she couldn't just leave the bags untied and walk away. They might fall over and spill their contents out on the ground and then Earl would have to clean it all up.

And *that* wouldn't be right.

'What are you doing?'

Emmy turned to see Samira.

'I've been watching you from my bedroom,' Samira said. 'You look like you need some help.'

Emmy explained her problem. Samira had the answer.

'We both press down at the same time,' she said, 'and then *I'll* hold the bag down while *you* make a knot.'

'Good idea,' Emmy said. She took off her gloves and gave them to Samira. 'But you'll need to wear these so your hands don't get dirty.'

They soon had all three bags tied up tight and neatly stacked beside the gates. Emmy let out a sigh of relief.

Her victory was short-lived.

Because when she looked back down at the

park and the pond, all she saw was everything she *hadn't* cleaned up. Yes, she'd got rid of the rubbish on the grass and at the edge of the water, but she hadn't touched anything *in* the pond. It was still as full of cans and crates and shopping trolleys as ever.

It still looked awful.

She felt like giving up and going home.

Samira didn't.

'I've got an idea,' she said.

12   Not Butterflies

Samira took Emmy back to her house. She opened the door to the tiny shed at the bottom of the garden.

It was packed with boxes and bicycles and gardening tools. Hanging in the corner was a long wooden pole with a net on the end. Samira pulled it down.

'It looks like a butterfly net,' Emmy said.

'It *is* a butterfly net,' Samira said.

'How's catching butterflies going to help us?' Emmy asked.

'Not *butterflies*,' Samira said. 'Tin cans. We can use the net to fish out the cans we can't reach from dry land.' She stepped outside and waved it back and forth. 'It's definitely long enough.'

'Won't your mum miss it?' Emmy asked.

Samira shook her head. 'She won't miss anything.'

'Why not?'

'Because she's sad.'

'Why's she sad?'

Samira took a long time to answer. Now she looked sad too. 'Because she's all on her own. My dad left us and didn't come back and she's been sad ever since. She never does anything. She certainly doesn't use *this*,' she added, holding up the net.

'I live with my uncle,' Emmy said. 'He's sad too.' She explained why.

The two girls stood on the grass and thought about Samira's mum and Emmy's uncle.

'It must be awful being grown-up and sad,' said Emmy. 'At least when you're little you've got toys to play with.'

'Cleaning up the pond might make Mum happy,' Samira said. 'She used to like to go there. And walk around.'

'Then let's go and do it for you mum,' Emmy said.

'And your uncle,' Samira said.

'I'm not sure anything would cheer my uncle up,' Emmy sighed. 'But we could always try, couldn't we?'

The two girls ran back to the park to start fishing tin cans out of the water. The net was too heavy for just one of them to hold, so they stood side by side and, using all four hands, were able to swing it out over the water.

It was hard going at first. It took them a long time to learn to use it effectively. But when they did, they were soon snatching up can after can. They made a pile of them on the grass.

By the time they'd worked their way all around the pond, the grass was dotted with little piles of cans and all sorts of other rubbish they'd caught in the net.

They opened a fourth plastic bag and began piling it all in. The bag filled up before they were even a quarter of the way round, because the cans took up so much space. So they emptied them out and stamped them flat with their feet. Then all the cans fitted into one bag. They tied it shut and carried it up to the gates to set it beside the others.

As they did so, Emmy spotted somebody watching them from the far side of the park. When he saw her looking, he ducked down behind a bush.

Samira saw him too.

'It's Neddy,' she said. '*Neddy the Elephant.*'

13   Neddy the Elephant

Neddy the Elephant was the name the Blascoe

Brothers had given him. They called him that because of

his big ears, and the fact that he was tall. He was almost

as tall as a few of the teachers.

'He's even as *big* as an elephant!' the Blascoe

Brothers shouted.

Like all the nicknames the brothers thought up,

this one stuck. Everyone started calling him *Neddy the*

Elephant. And then, because he was shy to start with,

this only made him shyer still. So he went everywhere

with his shoulders hunched and his head down,

avoiding people's eyes.

He was avoiding Emmy's eyes now. And

Samira's.

'I shouldn't call him that,' Samira said. 'It's not

nice. His real name's Michael. Michael Lau.'

'Then let's invite him over,' Emmy said.

The two girls waved at Michael and called out for him to come and join them, but he didn't. He stayed watching them from the safety of the rhododendron bush and refused to emerge.

'Perhaps if we leave him alone he'll come and join us,' Emmy said. 'Because I bet he could help us fish those plastic crates out of the water. He's much taller than either of us.'

The girls had tried pulling the crates from the pond, but their arms weren't long enough and they couldn't reach. So the two of them stood at the edge of the pond and made a big show of *not* looking at Michael Lau, hoping this would encourage him to come out of hiding. They were so busy *not* looking that they didn't notice who *was* creeping up on them.

Before they knew it, a massive splash had

soaked them from head to foot. Dripping with

duckweed, they spun round.

To find themselves face to face with the Blascoe

Brothers.

14 Surprise!

With a yell, the three brothers darted forward.

The girls turned and ran.

The brothers chased them all the way round the pond, up to the gates and out onto the street. Then they grabbed a plastic bag of rubbish each, ran back to the pond and threw all three into the water.

They weren't finished though.

Bash Blascoe spotted the butterfly net, grabbed it and pitched it into the air like a javelin. It landed in the middle of the pond with a splash and stood upright in the mud, swaying gently back and forth.

'What do you think of *that*?' he chortled, jumping up and down in triumph.

Emmy and Samira stood by the gates, staring sadly at all their ruined work. And the net they'd lost.

How were they going to explain that to Samira's mum? Both of them were ready to give up and go home.

But then Emmy remembered her dream.

She remembered the storm and the churning waves, and how Ariel had plunged straight into them without a second's hesitation.

'Bullies are always shouting and roaring and making tons of noise,' she'd said. 'I just ignore them. Then they don't know what to do. They get terribly confused.'

Emmy turned to Samira.

'No,' she said. 'They're not going to get away with it. I'm not going to let them scare me this time.'

She squared her shoulders, lifted her head and marched back into the park.

15   A Challenge

Ignoring her trembling knees and her pounding heart, Emmy marched all the way round the pond until she was face to face with the brothers. Bash Blascoe pretended to be scared and held his hands up in front of him, as though he were begging for mercy.

'Oh, don't hurt me, Smelly Emmy,' he pleaded. '*Please* don't hurt me.'

Emmy didn't reply.

She just stood still and looked at them.

The brothers were puzzled. This wasn't what usually happened. What *usually* happened was that kids got scared and ran away from them. They didn't stand there in silence and *stare*.

'Well?' Bash demanded.

'Well what?' Emmy asked.

'What do you *want*?' Brick said.

'Oh,' Emmy said, 'I was just thinking.'

Now the brothers were even *more* puzzled. Especially when Emmy didn't explain. They looked at her, waiting for her to continue. They'd forgotten all about chasing her by now and just wanted to know what was going on.

Finally, Bang couldn't take it anymore. He stamped his feet up and down with frustration. '*What* are you thinking?' he shouted.

Emmy folded her arms across her chest and turned to look at the butterfly net sticking up out of the mud.

'I was *thinking*,' she said at last, 'that you wouldn't be able to get that net back. So I was wondering how *I'm* going to do –'

'*Who* says we can't get it back?' Bash

demanded.

Emmy kept her arms folded and her breathing as calm as possible. Because this was the dangerous part. If what she said didn't work, the brothers would just turn around and leave.

'Oh,' she replied. 'Me and Samira. And probably *everyone else* at school when we tell them. They'll all come and look at the pond and see the butterfly net and know you couldn't rescue it. And then they'll all say how useless you all were.'

The brothers blinked.

They shook their heads.

'We're not useless,' they said.

They rolled up their sleeves and turned towards the pond.

'And we'll *prove* it!'

16   Puzzled. *Really* Puzzled

The brothers paced up and down on both sides of the pond, trying to decide how to retrieve the butterfly net.

'Are you stuck?' Emmy asked.

'Do you need some help?' Samira chimed in. Emmy being brave had made her feel brave too. She'd walked back into the park to join her friend.

'I can always go and ask my uncle,' Emmy said. 'I bet he'd know what to do.'

'We can *do* it!' the brothers replied. They'd completely forgotten about being bullies and chasing the girls out of the park. All they were thinking about now was rescuing the net and proving they weren't useless.

Bash snapped his fingers. 'I know what we do!'

he said. 'We lasso it.'

Brick and Bang didn't understand.

'We get a rope,' Bash said, 'and we make a noose and we throw it around the net and pull it back.'

Brick shook his head. 'But we haven't got a rope,' he said.

'Oh,' said Bash. His face fell. He hadn't thought about that.

'*We've* got one,' Samira said. 'In our garden shed. Shall I go and get it?'

The brothers hesitated. Were they going to let somebody *help* them? After what they'd said about it doing it all themselves? But it didn't take them long to realize, though, that they couldn't do it *without* Samira's help.

Reluctantly, they all nodded.

Samira dashed back home and returned with a

coil of rope over her shoulder. She handed it to the brothers. Bash fashioned a lasso and whirled it around his head. He sent it flying out over the water.

It missed.

It missed seven times in a row but, on the eighth attempt, the noose dropped down around the pole. Seconds later, Bash was wiping it clean with his handkerchief and handing it over to the girls.

'*Told* you we could get it back,' he announced.

All the three boys looked triumphant. It was obvious they were thinking: *look how great* we've *been*! But if they were expecting Emmy and Samira to argue with them, they were in for a shock.

'You certainly did,' Emmy said quietly. 'Thank you.'

'Yes,' Samira said. 'Thank you.'

The brothers were puzzled. *Really* puzzled. It

had been a long time since anybody had *thanked* them.

Teachers were always telling them to behave. Other

children were always running away from them. Nobody

had ever *thanked* them in absolutely ages.

It was *very* confusing.

But it was also rather nice.

It was so nice, in fact, that when the girls set to

work retrieving the rubbish bags and couldn't quite

reach the last one, the brothers stepped in to help. The

placed the bag on the grass with the others and handed

back the net.

'Thank you,' the girls said, which made the

brothers feel strange and tingly and nice all over again.

It made them feel *so* strange and tingly and nice

that instead of handing the net back, they used it to fish

all the plastic crates out of the pond as well.

And when they didn't leave, but stayed looking

at the pond and what they'd helped achieve, it gave

Emmy an idea.

'You know, I'm wondering,' she said. 'Do you

think we could get those shopping trolleys *out* too?'

17   Trolley Rescue

'Well, you can't use the net,' Bash said.

'It's not big enough,' Bang added.

'Or strong enough,' Brick concluded.

They sat down on the grass to think up a solution. Almost instantly, they jumped up.

'We'll lasso them, 'Bash said. 'Like we did the net.'

It seemed like a good idea, but it didn't work. They couldn't make a noose big enough to get a good grip on the trolleys. Every time they thought they'd succeeded and pulled, the rope slipped off into the water.

'It's like trying to catch a fish,' Samira said. 'It won't stay on the hook.'

All three brothers perked up. They raced away

out of the park without a word and returned with a bag of metal hooks.

'Dad uses them to hang things from the beams in his garage,' Bash explained. 'They save *tons* of space.'

He emptied the bag onto the grass and began sorting through the contents. He found a big blunt hook with a loop at one end. He threaded the rope through the loop and tied it tight.

It worked perfectly.

It landed on the handle of the trolley. And stayed there. Then all it took was five hard tugs from all three brothers to haul it up out of the water and onto dry land. While Emmy and Samira wheeled it away, the brothers started 'fishing out' the other trolleys. They rescued the second, then the third.

But they couldn't reach the last one.

Every attempt to land the hook fell short. It

splashed down uselessly in the water.

The five of them stood there, stumped.

'Can I help?'

The voice was so unexpected, it made *everyone* jump. They spun round to see Michael Lau. He'd crept down from his hiding place in the bushes and was watching them shyly. When nobody answered straight away – because they were too startled to talk – he blushed and ducked his head and turned to go.

Emmy grabbed his hand.

'Of *course* you can,' she said. 'You're probably just what we need. You're much taller than any of us.'

Still blushing, and not looking directly at any of them, Michael took the rope in his hands. He swung it back and forth to get used to it, then let it fly. It landed on the trolley the very first time. Then, before anyone could help him, he pulled it all the way out of the pond

.

by himself. He made it look as though it weighed less than a feather.

'*That*,' said Bash, staring at him with open admiration, 'was *seriously* cool!'

Michael hung his head and blushed even more furiously. But he didn't leave.

'Um,' Bash began. 'Sorry we called you Neddy the Elephant. It wasn't nice.'

Brick and Bang nodded their agreement.

Michael blushed again. Then he glanced at each brother in turn. 'What are *you* called?' he asked at last. 'Your real names, I mean.'

'Yes,' said Emmy. 'I'd like to know that too.'

'And me,' Samira said.

'I'm Ben,' Bash said.

'I'm Bobby,' Bat said.

'And I'm Brad,' Brick said.

'And we're sorry we called you names too,' Ben said to the girls. 'That wasn't nice either.'

'That's okay,' Emmy said. She rather liked the brothers now. She certainly wasn't scared of them. 'But you know, I think Bash is a much cooler name than Ben.'

Bash's face lit up with pride. 'You really think so?' he asked.

'Oh yes,' Emmy said. 'And Bang and Brick too. *Much* cooler.'

'But we don't want to be Smelly Emmy or Soppy Sammy again,' Samira said. '*Or* Neddy the Elephant.'

'We'll never let *anyone* call you that *ever* again,' Bash said.

The six children, now friends, stood at the edge of the pond and studied the results of all their hard work. It was still full of duckweed, but at least it looked like a proper pond, and not a place for everyone to dump their rubbish. As if to prove it, two ducks

fluttered down out of the sky and landed in the water in

front of them with a splash. They paddled back and

forth, quacking happily to each other.

Emmy watched them, then lifted her gaze to

the tree on the little island and all the plastic bags stuck

in the branches.

'If we could clean *them* up,' she said, 'it would

look even better.'

'Well, you won't have to,' announced a voice

from behind them. 'Because after tomorrow, there

won't *be* a tree. Or a pond. Or even a park.'

18   Bad News

The children turned to see a man and a woman wearing shiny yellow jackets. The man's arms were full of wooden posts. The woman was carrying a hammer and a big roll of yellow plastic tape. The name tag on the man's jacket said *E.Batt.* The tag on the woman's jacket said *R.Bunce.*

Emmy was the first to speak. 'What do you mean, there won't be a park?'

'What *I'd* like to know,' Mr Batt said, completely ignoring her question, 'is what you lot are doing here.'

'Cleaning the pond,' Emmy said, pointing to the bags of rubbish, the plastic crates and the four shopping trolleys.

'Cleaning the pond?' Mr Batt spluttered. 'Who said you could do that?'

'Nobody,' Samira said.

'It was full of rubbish,' Bash said. 'Now it isn't.'

Mr Batt and Ms Bunce were shocked.

'But it could have been dangerous,' Mr Batt said.

'You might have fallen in,' Ms Bunce said.

'Wouldn't have mattered if we had,' Emmy said. 'The pond's got more mud than water in it. If we'd fallen in, all we would have got was dirty.'

'And that is *precisely*,' Mr Batt announced, 'the reason we're getting rid of it. Do you see that?' he demanded, pointing at something behind them.

The children turned to stare at the hulk of a fallen tree. It had landed in the pond off to one side and was now a tangle of broken branches and clumps of grass and weeds.

'When that tree fell down,' Mr Batt went on, 'it

blocked the way out for the water. It *used* to flow into a stream that led to the cliffs and from there down to the sea.'

'But with the tree in the way,' Ms Bunce continued, 'there was no escape for the water that came from *that*.' She pointed to a large round pipe on the other side of the pond, opposite the tree. 'So the council shut the pipe and stopped the water.

'Why didn't somebody just take the tree away?' Emmy asked. 'Then the pond could have gone on being a pond.'

Mr Batt coughed and spluttered. 'I don't think it's up to little girls to question the decision of the town council,' he said. 'The *mayor's* decision is final.'

'If I were the mayor,' Ms Bunce said, looking a little dreamy, 'I'd put in lots of flowers.' Then she shook her head, as if to clear away such silly thoughts. 'But I'm not,' she said, 'so I won't. Mr Batt is right: what the mayor says goes.

'Grown-ups know *best*,' he announced.

He drew himself up his full height and held out one of the wooden posts, to which was fixed a bright yellow plastic square. Printed on it in bold red letters was the following announcement:

CONSTRUCTION WORK IN PROGRESS

AUTHORISED PERSONNEL ONLY

By order of Wilmington Council

'This is no longer a matter for children,' he said. 'So it's time to run along home. All of you. This area is now *closed*!'

With Ms Bunce's help, he began hammering the signs into the grass and stringing yellow plastic tape through the railings. When they'd finished, they shepherded the children out through the gates and onto the pavement.

'Take a good look,' Ms Bunce told them, 'because by this time tomorrow there'll be nothing to see but a nice, flat, *tidy* space.'

'But there won't be a *pond*,' Emmy protested.

Neither grown-up bothered to reply. They were too busy trying to close and lock the gates. But the gates were old and neglected and wouldn't shut properly. So Mr Batt and Ms Bunce wound yellow plastic tape back and forth across the opening to close it off.

'Work begins tomorrow,' Mr Batt said. 'At nine 'o clock sharp.'

'You're welcome to watch, of course,' Ms Bunce added.

The children watched them go. Nobody said anything. They were too sad to say anything. One by one, the boys and Samira drifted off back to their homes. Emmy watched them leave and then she went home too. She ate her supper in silence and went to bed. And in the night she dreamed.

It was an awful dream.

19 Ariel Silent

She was back in the pond, the very same pond she and her friends had cleaned that afternoon.

In the middle floated Ariel, lying on her back, drifting lazily back and forth. As Emmy watched, other sprites popped into view. They looked identical to their sister and soon there were thousands of them - millions even – all floating on their backs in the still, silent water.

And all of them were made of nothing but discarded rubbish.

A clap of thunder rumbled overhead. A thick, oily rain began to fall. As Emmy watched, the water sprites began to break apart. They dissolved into a sluggish sea of drinking straws and cola cans, shopping bags and plastic cups and takeaway boxes and bottle tops.

Ariel was the last to go.

She went in silence. She couldn't speak because her mouth was plugged by a plastic bag. All she had time for was last pleading look with her bottle top eyes. And then all that was left was a thick carpet of rubbish that stretched from horizon to horizon under a dark, thunderous sky.

Emmy woke up, trembling.

Early morning sunlight was streaming through the window.

She knew what she had to do.

20   Alone, But Not for Long

She dressed and tiptoed downstairs. She didn't want to wake her uncle. He might stop her.

She went out to the garden and fetched the wheelbarrow from the shed. Into the wheelbarrow went a plastic flowerpot, a garden chair, a pile of old sacks, a rake and a lamp with a broken shade. She wheeled them all to the front of the house, went back inside and collected paper, scissors, a roll of Sellotape and a fistful of felt tip pens.

She wrote a short message to her uncle, then took a banana and an apple from the bowl on the sideboard, filled an empty milk bottle with water and set off. The sun was up and the birds were singing. Because it was Sunday, the streets were empty. When she reached the park, she set down the barrow and got to work.

She put the lamp stand on one side of the gates and the flowerpot on the other. She filled the flower pot with sacks and stood the rake up in it. Then she put the paper on the ground and began to write in the biggest letters she could manage. She used several colours for each letter.

When she was finished, she used the Sellotape to fix one sheet of paper to the lampshade and another sheet to the tines of the rake. Then she slipped between the yellow tape Ms Bunce had wound across the gap in the gates the day before, and fixed a sheet of paper to each of the four signs he had hammered into the grass.

Finally, she lifted the garden chair from the wheelbarrow, patted off the dust and sat down. It was a little too big for her – her feet couldn't quite touch the ground – but that was all right. She wasn't planning to go anywhere for quite some time.

As she took the banana from her pocket and began to eat, two boys delivering newspapers rode past on their bikes. They skidded to a halt and stared.

They saw a little girl sitting on a large chair in front of the entrance to the park. She was surrounded by six hand-written signs in several different colours. They all said the same thing:

SAVE OUR POND!

IT'S THE ONLY ONE WE'VE GOT

The boys read them all, shrugged and rode off without a word.

Emmy's heart sank. She hadn't expected to be ignored like that. It made her wonder whether she was doing the right thing. Perhaps she was just being silly. Perhaps everybody who walked or rode or drove past would read her signs and ignore her. Perhaps all her work would be for *nothing*.

Her gloomy thoughts were interrupted by a question.

'What's going to happen to the pond?'

Emmy looked up to see an old lady walking a small dog.

'The council's going to fill it in,' Emmy said. She repeated everything Mr Batt and Ms Bunce had told her the day before.

The old lady shook her head. 'And it used to be such a nice pond, too,' she said. 'I remember it from when I was young. And I've watched it fill up with rubbish all these years and never done anything to keep it clean.'

'I was cleaning it yesterday,' Emmy said. 'With my friends.'

The old lady shook her head again. 'How sad,' she said. 'How sad.'

And away she walked.

Now Emmy felt *really* gloomy. She was convinced she was going to sit here all by herself and be ignored all day and end up going home looking like a complete and total fool. She hung her head and tried not to cry.

The sound of approaching footsteps made her look up.

The old lady with the dog was returning. She held the dog's lead in one hand and a small folding chair in the other. She set the chair down beside Emmy and settled herself in it. The dog sniffed Emmy's feet, then lay down beside her owner and put her head on her paws.

'My name is Veronica,' said the old lady. 'And

this young feller,' she added with a wave of her hand at the dog, 'is Ainsley.'

'I'm Emmy,' said Emmy.

'Very pleased to meet you, Emmy,' said Veronica. 'Now, tell me all about how you were cleaning the pond.'

So Emmy did. When she finished, Veronica reached into her pocket and took out her mobile.

Right!' she said, with a note of grim determination, 'I think it's time to call some friends.'

21   Friends Arrive

Veronica's first call was to a lady named Angelina. The volume was turned up so high that Emmy could hear every word both women said.

'Hello, dear,' Veronica said. 'Are you busy at the moment?

'I'm just having breakfast.'

'Well, put your shoes on and come down to the pond.'

Angelina sounded astonished. 'Now? But I've just buttered my toast.'

'Excellent,' replied Veronica. 'Bring it with you.'

'But why should I come down the pond?'

'Because there's a young lady here who needs our help.'

'What sort of help?'

'You'll find out when you get here. Hurry up, Angelina. No time to waste.'

She ended the call. 'Angelina can be such an old ditherer,' she said. 'Toast, indeed. Now, who else can I call?' She scrolled through her contacts and smiled. 'Why yes, of course!'

Her thumbs flew over the keys as she typed a message. She pressed *Send* and sat back with a satisfied smile.

'That should liven things up,' she said.

Emmy soon found out why. At the end of the street, an elderly lady appeared. She was leading two corgi dogs on separate leads. When they got close enough to catch Ainsley's scent, they began to bark and wag their tails. Soon all three dogs were scampering back and forth, getting their leashes in knots as they said hello to each other.

91

Things soon calmed down. But no sooner had they settled on the ground at their owners' feet than two more women appeared from the other end of the street. They were both leading dogs as well: a Jack Russell and a bull terrier.

Chaos ensued once again as Ainsley and the corgis jumped up to greet the new arrivals. By now the entrance to the park was filled with barking dogs wagging their tails and four owners chattering away happily to each other. The last to arrive was Angelina. She came tapping along with the aid of a walking stick.

'And just *why*,' she demanded as she reached them, 'have you called me here, Veronica?'

'This young lady,' Veronica said, gesturing to Emmy, 'needs our help.' She told them about the pond and Emmy's efforts to clean it, and how work would start at nine o'clock.

Veronica's friends were shocked.

'Fill in the pond?' said the woman with the corgis.

'On a *Sunday*?' said the owner of the Jack Russell

'Without telling anyone first?' added the lady with the bull terrier.

'Shocking!' Angelina said. 'Intolerable! And just when it's beginning to look so nice too.'She turned to look at Emmy. 'Well done you,' she said.

'Oh,' Emmy said, 'I didn't do it on my own. My friends helped too.'

'Well, you did a very good job,' Angelina said. 'And it deserves to be protected.' The handle of her walking stick opened out to make a seat. She plonked herself down on it and folded her arms across her chest. 'They'll not be filling anything in while *I'm* here.'

By now it was almost nine o' clock. Three ducks flew down over the houses and landed in the pond with a soft splash. They paddled back and forth, quacking happily.

But soon another sound began to drown them out.

It was the rumble of heavy vehicles. The very ground under everyone's feet began to shudder and Emmy and her new friends looked up to see a convoy of trucks and a bright yellow bulldozer approaching.

At the head of the procession was a small car. In the car, behind the wheel, was Mr Batt. Beside him sat Ms Bunce. The car stopped in front of the gates and they both stepped out.

'And just what,' demanded Ms Bunce, 'is going on here?'

'You're blocking the entrance,' said Mr Batt.

'Full marks for observation,' Veronica said. 'It speaks highly of civil service recruitment.'

'But what are you *doing*?' Ms Bunce repeated.

'Helping this young lady protect the park,' replied Veronica. 'And all her hard work cleaning out the pond.'

'Well, you're wasting your time,' said Mr Batt. 'Neither of them will be here by the end of the day. The park's being levelled and the pond's being filled in.'

'Really?' said Veronica. 'And how do you intend to do that?'

Mr Batt pointed to the line of vehicles behind him. 'With those,' he said.

Veronica nodded. 'And how are they going to get *into* the park?' she wondered.

'Through this gate,' said Ms Bunce.

'I don't think so,' said Veronica.

'Why not?' asked Mr Batt.

'Because *we*,' Veronica said, with a wave of her hand that encompassed Emmy, Angelina, the other three dog owners and the dogs themselves, 'aren't moving.'

'But you *have* to move!' Mr Batt and Ms Bunce cried.

'Oh no, we don't,' replied Veronica. She turned to her friends. 'Isn't that right, girls?'

All the old ladies nodded in agreement.

'We'll see about that!' Mr Batt said and strode off with Ms Bunce to talk to the driver of the bulldozer.

Emmy watched them stop beside it. The driver jumped down to talk to them. After a few words had been exchanged, the driver turned to stare at the crowd in front of the gates, and at Emmy in particular. He said something to Mr Batt and Ms Bunce and they nodded.

The driver reached up and switched off the bulldozer's engine.

He started walking towards the park.

He was a big man, far taller than anybody else in the street. He had a shaved head, a massive beard and a T-shirt bulging with muscles. As he drew closer and closer to the gates, everyone stopped talking and watched him approach. Even the dogs fell silent.

Emmy knew what was going to happen. He was going to pick her up, carry her away and then drive the bulldozer right into the park.

Instead he stopped before her and demanded, in a rumbling voice so deep it made her tummy tremble, 'Is your name Emmy?'

'Yes,' Emmy said. The word came out as a squeak.

The bulldozer driver smiled a smile that lit up

every inch of his face and stuck out his hand.

'I am *so* pleased to meet you!' he said.

22 A Complete Change

'Pleased to meet me?' said Emmy, totally confused.

'Oh, yes,' the bulldozer driver said. 'My name's Alec, you see. Alec Blascoe.'

Emmy's eyes widened.

'And Ben, Bobby and Brad are my sons,' he said. 'They came home yesterday and it was like I was opening the door to three different people. People I hadn't seen in *ages*.'

Emmy was even more confused.

'Their mum's been ill,' Alec explained. 'She's been in the hospital for months now, and I've been visiting her every day. And because I've been doing that, I've been neglecting my boys. I haven't spent enough time with them. I've let them do what they like. And they've become little terrors. All three of them.'

His face grew sad.

'I knew it was happening,' he went on. 'But I kept telling myself I'd be able to sort them out when things got better with their mum. Only, she didn't get better and the boys got worse and I was at my wit's end wondering if they'd ever get back to being the nice young boys they used to be. And then they met you. What did you *say* to them?'

Emmy hesitated. She didn't want to tell the boys' dad *everything* they'd done yesterday. That might just get them in more trouble. So she said, 'I just bet them they couldn't rescue a butterfly net that had got caught in the mud. But they could. And then when they'd done that, I said wouldn't it be great if they could help pull the shopping trolleys out too. And they did that too. They helped me and my friend Samira tidy up

100

the park. That's all really.'

Alec scratched his head. 'Well, it certainly had a _big_ effect on them. They came home yesterday and tidied up their rooms without me having to ask them once. And then they helped with the washing up and went to bed on time. It was such a change I almost felt like calling the doctor.'

Emmy peered around him, looking for the brothers.

'Oh, they're not with me,' Alec said. 'They're cleaning up the garden shed, like I asked them to three months ago. They'll be along when they're finished.' He looked past her and into the park. 'You all certainly did a good job with it. I've never seen it looking so tidy.'

All this time he'd been carrying a large canvas bag on his shoulder. Now he put it down and opened it up to take out a thermos flask.

'I could do with a good cup of tea,' he said. 'I went to the hospital first thing this morning to see my wife and this is the first chance I've had for a drink. I haven't got any extra cups though,' he added, looking around at the people assembled in front of the gates.

'That's all right,' said a voice behind him. 'We have.'

Everyone turned to see a man and a woman crossing the road carrying two trays crammed with mugs and a second thermos.

'We've been listening to everything that's going on,' the woman said. 'I'm Agnes. This is my husband, Derek. We thought you could all use some refreshment. I think what this young lady did yesterday was excellent!' she added, nodding at Emmy and doling out mugs. 'It's made such a difference to the park.'

'It wasn't just me,' Emmy said. 'My friends

helped me.'

But nobody seemed to hear that. They were too busy enjoying their tea and biscuits. Soon everyone was chatting with everyone else and the air was filled with the sound of voices and laughter as they all got to know one another.

Until a very loud cough interrupted the proceedings. Everyone turned to see Mr Batt and Ms Bunce. They both looked very impatient.

'Isn't it *time*,' Mr Batt demanded of Alec, 'that you got to work?'

Alec's face grew serious. He put away his cup and his thermos flask and closed the bag he carried them in.

'Yes,' he said quietly. 'Yes, of course.' He turned to everyone gathered in front of the gates. 'You'd better all move,' he told them. 'Just to be safe.'

Ignoring the looks of astonishment and disappointment, he ripped away the yellow tape and pushed the gates wide open. Then he set off back to the bulldozer.

Emmy was distraught. 'But you can't!' she shouted. 'You *can't!*'

Alec ignored her. He stopped to talk a man in blue overalls before climbing up onto the bulldozer and starting the engine. Smoke billowed from the exhaust pipe. The massive iron monster rumbled forward. Everyone in front of the gates watched as it approached before scrambling to get out of the way.

It didn't go into the park though. It stopped between the gates, leaving a gap on one side just big enough for people to squeeze through one at a time. Alec switched off the engine and jumped down from the driver's seat.

'You're right,' he said, walking up to Mr Batt and Ms Bunce. 'It *is* time to get to work. It's time to help young Emmy here.'

'Help her do what?' Mr Batt spluttered.

'What she started yesterday,' Alec said. 'Cleaning up this pond.' He turned to Emmy. 'So why don't you tell me what we still have to do?'

23   The Final Obstacle

Emmy showed him the tree blocking the pond.

'It's like a dam,' she said. 'Especially with all the weeds and rubbish clogging up the bottom half.'

'So if we could get rid of it,' Alec said, 'there'd be somewhere for the water in the pond to go.'

Emmy smiled and nodded, happy that Alec understood.

'But we didn't get the chance to try,' she said. 'And besides, we wouldn't have been big enough anyway. Not to get rid of a whole tree.'

Alec returned her smile. 'Well, we aren't.'

'*We*?' Emmy asked.

Alec turned and pointed to the man walking across the grass towards them. It was the man in blue overalls he'd been speaking to earlier. He was carrying two sets of waders, a tool box and a large rope slung round his shoulders. Behind him came Bash, Bang and Brick. Bash was carrying a large cardboard box.

'This is my friend Malik,' Alec said. 'Malik Iqbal. We work together.'

The man in blue overalls shook Emmy's hand. 'Pleased to meet you, Emmy,' he said. 'Wonderful what you've done here.'

'What I've done with my friends,' Emmy said.

But Malik didn't hear her. He was busy climbing into his waders. Alec did the same. Together they stepped down into the muddy water and waded over to the fallen tree. After a few minutes mulling the problem over, they pulled on long rubber gloves and began hauling dead branches and weeds out of the water. They threw everything onto the bank.

'Okay, lads,' Alec said to his sons. 'Now you can

get started.'

Bash opened the box he'd been carrying and took out a roll of rubbish bags and four pairs of gloves. One pair for each boy and one for Emmy. They put them on and began bagging the rubbish and stacking the broken branches neatly.

'How's your mum?' Emmy asked as they worked.

'She's getting better,' Bash said.

'Should be leaving hospital next week,' Bang said.

'And this'll be a nice surprise for her,' Brick added. 'Seeing the pond back again.'

They worked on steadily and, while they did, the ladies who'd helped Emmy start her protest strolled down to watch. The first to arrive was Veronica. She was laughing. Emmy asked her why.

'Because you're collecting money,' Veronica said. 'A man walked past, saw your signs and said he couldn't stop. But he put five pounds in the flower pot because he thought it was a collection. And then others did too. There's fifty pounds already.'

And people weren't just donating money. The park was filling up with spectators, all using their mobiles to record the work on the tree. Veronica's mobile kept pinging as new messages flooded in.

'Oh, my dear young Emmy,' she smiled. 'You really have started something, you know. This is all over social media.' She held out her phone and flicked through all the sites carrying the story of what was happening in the park. 'You should be proud of yourself.'

'It wasn't just me,' Emmy repeated. 'My friends helped too.'

But her words were drowned out as Malik produced a small chain saw and began cutting up the tree trunk. Alec hauled the pieces away and Bash, Brick and Bang stacked them up too. The pile of wood had grown almost as tall as Emmy.

She gazed across a park now filled with people of all ages, chatting away to each other or talking on their mobiles or taking pictures. Others were sharing cups of tea and bottles of water. Three people had managed to get a ladder onto the little island and were using it to tug the plastic bags from the branches.

The air was filled with the sound of laughter and voices and the happy barks of dogs galloping back and forth. It was absolutely wonderful and quite the last thing she had ever imagined when she woke up that morning.

But the surprises weren't over yet.

Up on the road, a yellow van had pulled up beside the gates. Two women stepped out. One was smartly dressed and holding a microphone. The other was wearing jeans and a T-shirt, and carrying a video camera on her shoulder. They entered the park and marched across the grass. Emmy could hear the smartly-dressed woman calling out her name.

'Emmeline Townsend? Has anyone seen Emmeline Townsend?'

Emmy held up her hand.

'That's me,' she said.

'Oh, good!' smiled the woman. 'How *lovely* to meet you. I'm Laura Righthop and I'm from the BBC. I've come to interview you.'

24   A Local Celebrity

Emmy was so surprised she could barely speak.

'*Interview* me?' she said. 'What about?'

'Rescuing this pond, of course,' said Laura Righthop.

'Oh, it wasn't just me,' Emmy said. 'I had lots of help from my friends. You should talk to them too.'

'It's all over social media,' Laura Righthop said. 'Everyone's talking about young Emmy saving the pond.'

'But it *wasn't* just me,' Emmy insisted. 'My friends helped too. And then everyone who came today.'

Laura Righthop was conferring with the camerawoman. She turned back to Emmy

'What we'd like to do, 'she said, 'is interview

you live. We can start in a minute. They're all ready in the studio. All you have to do is stand right where you are and answer my questions.'

'Can my friends be interviewed too?' Emmy asked. 'They helped just –'

'No, no,' Laura Righthop said. 'Just you. We've only got time to interview one person.'

She pressed her finger to the microphone in her ear, listening to someone speaking to her from the studio. Then a light turned red on the camera and the woman holding gave Laura Righthop a thumbs up.

The interview began.

'I'm standing here in Pennsdale Park in the seaside town of Wilmington, talking to eight-year-old Emmeline Townsend, a young lady who has single-handedly turned an untidy, deserted eyesore into the neat and tidy beauty spot you can now see emerging behind us.'

The camera moved away from Emmy to take in the clean grass and the litter-free pond. When it swung back, Laura Righthop held the microphone in front of Emmy.

'So how did it all start, Emmy?' she asked. 'What made you decide to take action?'

'It was just so dirty,' Emmy said, surprised to discover that she didn't feel nervous at all. 'And I thought, the least I could do was pick up all the plastic bags. And then when I'd done that, I thought it would be great if I could grab all the tin cans in the water. And a friend helped me do that. And then more friends helped me drag the plastic crates and shopping trolleys out. That's how we did it.'

'Excellent,' Laura Righthop said. 'But you wanted to do more didn't you? You didn't stop there.'

'No,' Emmy said. 'When I heard they were going to fill the whole park in, I thought that wasn't right. All it needed was tidying up. Not filling in.'

'So you started a one-girl protest,' Laura Righthop said.

Emmy nodded.

'Were you scared?'

'A little bit at first,' Emmy said, 'when I was all alone. But then people arrived and when they found out what I was doing and why, they said they'd stay and help me. So I wasn't alone anymore. So there wasn't any reason to be scared.'

'And now you're a hero on social media. People are all talking about you. How does that feel? Is it fun being famous?'

'Oh, no,' Emmy said. 'That's not important. It's the park that's important. Not *me*.'

Laura Righthop looked surprised, as though she couldn't understand why somebody didn't want to be famous. 'Really?' she said.

'Oh yes,' Emmy said. 'I'd be happy if everyone else went out and cleaned up *their* ponds. If everybody did just a little bit in their own world, think what a difference it could make. That would be *really* great.'

At that moment, a cheer went up from behind her. She turned to see the last piece of the tree trunk being cut in two. Malik and Alec and two more men used the rope to haul them both pieces out of the pond and up onto the bank.

The way was finally clear to the sea.

It was at that moment that a large, shiny black car pulled up beside the bulldozer. A man in suit stepped out. Emmy didn't recognize him, but Veronica did.

'It's the mayor,' she said, as he made his way

through the gates and across the grass towards Emmy.

Behind him, striding along and looking very

severe, were Mr Batt and Ms Bunce.

25 An Official Decision

Mr Batt and Ms Bunce led the mayor straight to Emmy.

'Here she is,' said Mr Batt.

'The troublemaker,' added Ms Bunce.

The mayor peered down at Emmy. 'Well, young lady,' he said. 'What have you got to say for yourself?'

Emmy, who by now had gotten used to being stared at by much bigger people, stared right back.

'I've cleaned up the park,' she said. 'Me and my friends.'

'And who gave you permission?' the mayor asked.

'Nobody!' said Mr Batt.

'Nobody at all!' said Ms Bunce.

'We didn't think we needed permission to tidy it

up,' Emmy said. 'Isn't that what people are supposed to do? Tidy up after themselves?'

'Well, yes, erm,' the mayor said. Emmy had caught him off guard by reminding him about something so simple. And he'd just realised that there was a camera filming him. He regained his composure and carried on. 'But you can't go running around on your own, stirring up trouble and collecting crowds and interfering with council business.'

Mr Batt and Ms Bunce nodded vigorously in agreement.

'She *wasn't* alone,' said a voice at Emmy's back.

It was Veronica who'd spoken. Beside her stood Abigail. Beside Abigail stood Alec and Malik and the two other men who'd helped with the tree. And all around them were all the other people who'd come to the park. Everybody who'd either joined the protest at the gates or helped with clearing away the tree trunk.

'And who would you be, madam?' the mayor asked Veronica.

'Veronica Eloise McMillican Cartwright,' came the reply. 'And I think I speak for everyone here when I say that while it might have been everyone's fault for letting the park get *into* such a state, filling it in and pretending it never existed is *not* the answer.'

Everyone in the crowd nodded vigorously.

'Well, you should have done something sooner,' Mr Batt said.

'The council can't change its plans now,' Ms Bunce added.

'Is that right, Mr Mayor?'

The question had come from Laura Righthop. She was standing at the mayor's side, with her microphone in hand and the camera still filming.

'Is it *really* too late to change the council's

plans?' she went on. 'After all the work that's been

done today?'

The mayor coughed. He said, 'Hrmph' and 'Well'

and 'Er'.

'There's really only one thing left to do, you

know.'

It was Malik who'd spoken. The camera swung

towards him.

'And what would that be?' Laura Righthop

asked.

'Turn the water back on,' Malik said.

He pointed across the park to the dried-up pipe

poking out of the far bank under the iron fence. 'All you

have to do is clear those weeds out of the mouth and

turn the water back on and this pond'll fill up right

quick. And you wouldn't have to worry about it

flooding, because if there's too much water, it'll just flow away down the stream that tree blocked, and over the cliffs into the sea. Just like it used to.'

Laura Righthop turned to the mayor.

'Is that right, Mr Mayor?' she asked. 'Can the water be turned back on?'

Malik interrupted before the mayor could say a word.

'Course it can,' he said. 'And I should know.'

'Why?' asked Laura Righthop.

'Because I'm the one who turned it off in the first place, three years ago. All you've got to do is turn a wheel, open a valve and Bob's your uncle. A pond full of water.'

A murmur of excitement rippled through the crowd.

'A proper pond,' said a woman

'And ducks,' said another.

'And a *waterfall*,' said a third.

Silence fell as everyone in the crowd turned to look at the mayor. Laura Righthop held her microphone before him.

'What do you say, Mr Mayor?' she asked. 'What's your answer?'

The mayor turned to look at the crowd of people watching him. He said, 'Hrmph' and 'Well' and 'Er' again. Then he turned to Malik and said, 'I say, let's turn the water back *on*!'

26   A Smile

Malik set off straight away. While he was gone, Alec and the two men who'd helped with the tree began to clear the mud and weeds out of the mouth of the pipe. Laura Righthop went dashing back and forth, interviewing as many people as she could. Emmy didn't pay any attention though, because she'd just seen Samira running towards her.

'We saw you!' Samira gasped as she came to a breathless stop in front of her friend. 'We were visiting my granny. We always go on Sundays. Me and Mum. Granny turned on the telly and there you were. So we had to come back. As fast as we could. Isn't that right, Mum!'

She held out her hand to a tall, dark-haired woman with a tired face. Mrs Fakhoury looked down at

Emmy. 'I'm pleased to meet you,' she said. 'Samira hasn't stopped talking about you all the way back from my mother's. I didn't think she'd *ever* stop.'

She gazed around her, at the park and the pond and the pile of wood from the chopped-up tree trunk.

'It's really quite an achievement,' she said. 'You should be very proud of yourself.'

'It certainly is,' said a voice behind them. 'And so she should.'

Emmy turned to see her uncle making his way towards them. He'd shaved and brushed his hair and put on a smart suit, and he didn't look anything like the old, sad Uncle Glum anymore. Emmy thought he looked handsome and dashing.

'I saw you on the television,' he said to Emmy. 'A friend sent me a text and told me to turn it on and there you were. And then *more* friends sent *more* texts telling me to watch. In the end I thought it would be easier just to come down to the park to see for myself. Are you going to introduce me to your friends?' he asked.

Emmy made the introductions. Her uncle turned to Mrs Fakhoury and inclined his head in a small bow.

'كيفيك مدام فاخوري؟ كتير مبسوط إني إلتقيت فيكي' he said.

Mrs Fakhoury's eyes widened a little with surprise, and then she replied, 'بتحكي عربي؟'.

'بعرف شوي، عشت بلبنان أربع سنوات لما كنت صغير' he said.

'ماشاء الله كتير منيحة لهجتك', she said.

Emmy was staring wide-eyed with astonishment at her uncle. 'What did you just say?' she asked.

Samira explained. 'He said , 'How do you do, Mrs Fakhoury? I'm very pleased to meet you,' and Mum said, '*You speak Arabic?*' and then your uncle said, '*A little. I lived in Lebanon for four years, when I was younger.*' And then Mum said, '*Well, it's very good.*'

Her uncle turned to look at her. 'I learned it when I was a reporter,' he explained. 'It always helps to speak another person's language if you're a reporter.'

Then he turned back to Mrs Fakhoury and did something that left Emmy even more astonished.

He smiled.

And kept smiling.

To Samira's astonishment, her mum smiled back. And *she* kept smiling too.

Chatting happily in Arabic, the two grown-ups strolled away across the grass. The two girls would have stood there staring at them for ages if a sound from the other side of the park hadn't snapped them out of their little daze.

From the mouth of the pipe there came a long, gurgling cough.

The water was coming.

27   All Together

The cough was followed by a string of hisses and more coughs. Then came a roar. It sounded like a train rumbling through a tunnel.

As everyone in the park gathered round the pipe, a thin stream of dirty water gurgled into view. This was followed by a belch of damp, musty air and a trickle of clean water. The trickle became a stream. The stream became a steady wave that gushed from the mouth of the pipe.

In silence, everyone watched as it splashed down into the pond, breaking apart the carpet of duckweed for good and lifting the water level inch by inch. Up and up it rose, pushing ever closer to the channel that had until so recently been blocked by the fallen tree.

Laura Righthop came rushing up to Emmy.

'Right,' she said. 'It's your moment of triumph. Let's get a picture of you. Emmy, the saviour of the pond.'

Emmy shook her head. 'No.'

Laura Righthop frowned. 'Why not?"

'Because I didn't do it on my own,' Emmy said. 'I did it with my friends. *We're* the saviour of the pond.' She spread her arms wide, to take in everyone in the park, everyone who'd joined her protest. 'And I won't let you take a picture without them.'

She folded her arms and gave the reporter a defiant stare.

'Really?' Laura Righthop said.

'Really,' Emmy said.

She beckoned for Samira to stand beside her. And then Bash and Brick and Bang. She made everyone gather round, including her uncle and Mrs Fakhoury (both still chattering away in Arabic) and Earl who'd lent her the plastic bags and come along to see what was happening. When she spotted Michael Lau hovering in the background, she asked him to stand right beside her, instead of the mayor.

'Are we all ready?' Laura Righthop called out.

'Not yet,' Emmy said. She beckoned to two figures standing all the way off to one side. Both of them looked lost and left out.

It was Mr Batt and Ms Bunce.

'You too!' Emmy said.

'Us?' Mr Batt said.

'We didn't do anything,' Ms Bunce said.

'No,' Emmy said. 'But I bet you can. You can look after the pond. Now it's clean. You can make sure it *stays* clean. And there's all that money that got collected. You could use it to buy some flowers. You

131

said you liked flowers, didn't you, Ms Bunce?'

Ms Bunce's eyes lit up. 'Really?' she asked.

'Well, people did give that money to the park,' Emmy said. 'I don't think they'd mind if it got spent on flowers.'

Ms Bunce was really smiling now. She turned to Mr Batt. 'Oh, Ted,' she sighed, 'isn't that a wonderful idea? We could go to the garden centre and choose them together.'

Mr Batt blushed at being called Ted in public. But he smiled – a little – and joined Ms Bunce at the edge of the crowd.

'All together!' Laura Righthop called out. 'Everyone wave! And shout *water*!'

Everyone waved. 'Water!' they shouted, as loud and as hard as they could.

The camera captured the moment forever.

28   Goodbye

Emmy walked down to the park the next

morning. It had rained in the night, a gentle summer

rain that left a coating of dew on the grass and drops of

water falling from the leaves of the trees. A thin mist

hovered over the surface of the pond.

Everything was quiet and still.

She walked all the way round to the spot where

the tree had been removed. A thin, steady stream of

water now flowed past her, gurgling and chuckling on

its way towards the cliff and the waterfall waiting to

greet it.

That was when Emmy saw Ariel, drifting gently

along below the surface.

She looked the way she'd looked the night she'd

appeared outside Emmy's bedroom window. Her eyes

were no longer bottle tops. Her arms and legs weren't made of plastic. Her hair was once more a long, flowing mane of red.

When she saw Emmy, she looked up and waved. She turned a somersault and spun in happy circles.

'You did it,' she said. 'I knew you could.'

'And my friends,' Emmy said.

'And your friends,' Ariel agreed. She swayed back and forth in the current. 'But I have to go now,' she said. 'It's time for me to join *my* friends.'

As she spoke, a pair of beautiful wings unfolded from her back and spread out in the water.

'Will I see you again?' Emmy asked.

Ariel smiled. 'Of course,' she said. 'You brought me back to life, you know. You did your bit. I won't forget that for a second.'

She slipped into the stream, rolling and tumbling happily along as she picked up speed.

'Wheeeee!' she giggled. 'This is such *fun*!'

And with one final wave she was gone, over the edge of the cliff and away with the current, to the welcoming embrace of the distant waters, and all her friends and family far beyond.

Emmy smiled.

And then she went home for breakfast.

ABOUT THE AUTHOR

Nick Garlick was born in the UK but now lives in the Netherlands, near the city of Utrecht. He's written several books for children.

Aunt Severe and the Dragons
Aunt Severe and the Toy Thieves
Storm Horse
De Zusjes Jennifer (in Dutch)

The GFC (available as an eBook from Amazon)

Printed in Great Britain
by Amazon